FRESH PRINCESS

For magical little girls who dare to color outside the lines, filling our world with beauty, wonder, and light. We see you.—D.M.

To my mom, for allowing me to dream.
To Reno, for giving me the encouragement to dream.
And to Miranda, for being the reason that I dream.—G.J.

Fresh Princess
Copyright © 2019 by Treyball Content, LLC
All rights reserved. Printed in the United States of America.
No part of this book may be used or reproduced in any manner whatsoever without written permission
except in the case of brief quotations embodied in critical articles and reviews. For information address
HarperCollins Children's Books, a division of HarperCollins Publishers, 195 Broadway, New York, NY 10007.
www.harpercollinschildrens.com

ISBN 978-0-06-288457-2

The artist used Adobe Photoshop to create the digital illustrations for this book.
Design by Chelsea C. Donaldson
19 20 21 22 23 PC 10 9 8 7 6 5 4 3 2 1
❖
First Edition

FRESH PRINCESS

Written by Denene Millner
Illustrated by Gladys Jose

HARPER
An Imprint of HarperCollinsPublishers

This is Destiny.

Her dad calls her Princess.
His Fresh Princess.

Destiny likes a lot of the things that princesses like.

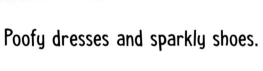

Poofy dresses and sparkly shoes.

Shiny crowns.

Her princess throne.
And her loyal subjects too.

She's also really good at being really fresh. That means she's brave, has her own style, and is supersmart. She shines like a new penny. Most days, being fresh is a good thing.

Like when Destiny's big sister, Marley, teaches her how to double Dutch, and Destiny jumps . . .

and trips . . .

and struggles . . .

and jumps back in again, cool as she pleases,
until she's got it licked.

Today, Fresh Princess is not feeling fresh at all. That's because her family is moving to a new house in a new city. It is far away from everyone she knows and everything she loves.

Destiny is *not* happy about that.

Her dad tries to make it all better. That is his thing.

Boo-boos get Band-Aids.

Bellyaches get soft rubs.

Sleepy heads get good-night kisses.

On this day, getting back to feeling joyful takes way more work. Her heart will need more to fill in the empty spaces where her happy used to be.

Destiny perks up a little bit when she sees her new room.
"It has potential," she says to herself.
She imagines the magnificent cities she'll build there, the
fancy luncheons she'll host, and the new throne that will be
the centerpiece of her new castle.

Destiny's Room

Destiny finds a new favorite place where the daylight greets her every morning

and the stars wink at her each night.

She perks up a little more when she looks outside.
Destiny listens to the rhymes as the double Dutch rope
skips a beat across the concrete.

Bluebells, cockleshells, evie ivy over!

The jumpers swing their hips. And watch the ropes.
Then they take flight. Destiny thinks it might be fun
to jump in, but those kids are good . . . *really* good.
So, for now, she just watches.

Her dad wants to help his Fresh Princess feel at home,
so he invites her on a big adventure.

One of his favorite things to do when he was a kid in this neighborhood was to ride the El train. "Speeding at the top of the city made me feel like the king of the world," Dad says. "Let's go see YOUR new kingdom."

"Madam, your royal carriage."
Destiny takes Dad's hand, climbs the steps, and prances down the aisle to her royal seat.

She giggles as the train picks up speed, whistling and whirring through West Philadelphia.

Along the way, Destiny's dad points out love letters tucked on the buildings' rooftops and spines. "Keep your head to the sky, Fresh Princess," he says as they roll on by.

THE BEST THINGS ARE ON THE OTHER SIDE OF FEAR

FIND YOUR MUSE

Destiny waves and blows kisses as the buildings salute her passing by.
She does love what she sees. But still, she aches for home.

Back at their new place, the kids are playing double Dutch again.
One of the girls flashes a smile and invites her to join.
Destiny says, "No thanks."

She is not ready for her public. Not yet. Maybe soon.

"Why are you not playing double Dutch?" asks Marley. "You are just as good a jumper as anybody here," she says with a smile.

"What if I fall flat on my face?" asks Destiny.

"It wouldn't be the first time. Plus you'd just get back up. You're the Fresh Princess."

Destiny thinks about this and realizes she *can* do it.
So she grabs her sparkly sneakers and decides to get out there
and show them how it's done!

"Can you jump?" asks one of the girls. She says her name is Mari.
Destiny gives a slow yes.
"Come jump with us!" says Mari.

Mari introduces Destiny to the block. There is Shani and
Esete. Zoe and Zion. Miles and two Lilas.

Finally, it's her go. Destiny takes her place next to the ropes as the turners swing their arms.

Cinderella, dressed in yella,
went upstairs to kiss her fella

Destiny takes a deep breath, swings her hips to the beat, and,
like the brave Fresh Princess, jumps in.

And the happiness she feels in this very moment, jumping high and free, surrounded by her new friends, is the freshest of all.